Beach times !
Fun times !

Nancy Usich
2006

Dear Phil,

Congratulations !

With most fond
memories of your
time here in
Avon —

Nancy.
07

Salt Water Kisses . . . A Nantucket "Tail"

Co-imagined by Kristen Usich & Nancy Usich

Illustrated by Amanda & Rusty Gibbs

A SALT WATER KISSES PUBLICATION
WWW. SALTWATERKISSES.COM

For Kristen, my only daughter, my best friend, my dream weaver.
—NRU

For my Parents Nancy & Bud, who taught me to live, love, and laugh and who made
"home" such a wonderful and happy place.
—KEU

Mermaid

her brilliance shines as she skims below the surface.

she possesses girlish qualities with a womanly depth of understanding, and the wisdom
of the oldest of souls.
she is playful but always learning.
she dances even when others cannot hear the music.
she explores but her curiosity is never satiated.
she seeks, unveils, and finds . . . but never what she yearns.
she is protected beneath her
blanket . . . peeking out for few.
she reveals herself only to the special and
true, and even more rare are those who truly
understand her mystique.

her silliness is laced with sadness, and her
crystal-like eyes shine with a childlike delight.

she has a smile that is sometimes uncertain, but
a laugh that is heart-filled and whole.
she is a beauty of unworldly measure.
she will touch your soul . . . and heart forever.
she skims beneath the surface . . . peeking out for few.
she is a gift from the sea . . . she is a mermaid.

—Kristen

"Hurry, Mom, I want to get to the top!" Mary Margaret rushed up the steep and narrow stairs that lead you away from the bottom of the cramped and noisy ferry to the spacious upper deck. Mary Margaret was way ahead of her mother.

She wanted the chair closest to the railing so that with a twist of her head she could watch the huge filled ferry slowly pull away from the dock. Hands covering her ears, she waited for the loud piercing sound of the goodbye horn. She watched the people waving from the main land grow smaller and smaller as her ferry set out to sea.

Her mother collapsed on the blue plastic chair and Mary Margaret's thumping heart told her the summer fun was about to begin.

Mary Margaret rummaged through the old stained canvas bag for the sandwich and snacks that she knew her mom had packed. She held the crusts of her unfinished sandwich high over her head and giggled as a seagull swooped to gently take them from her fingers and then fly away.

She waved to the passing sailboats and the passengers waved back, shouting, "Have a good trip!" The wind sometimes took their words away, but she knew by the smiles on their faces that they were wishing her something special.

Sometimes on the journey she would read from her favorite book, but other times it was hard to sit still long enough to read the chapters. Other times her stomach felt a little queasy as the words rolled together and off the page with the gentle back and forth rocking of the ferry.

5

She loved to lift her face to the wind and feel her hair wave behind her like the flags on the gigantic boats that she watched from the railing of the ferry. She closed her eyes and let the sun warm her cheeks, helping her forget the cold and snowy winter that was being left behind. Breathing deeply, she inhaled the salty air and knew that her very special time with her mother was about to begin.

The hardest part was the wait until she saw the rocks of the jetties, the weathered lighthouse, and the spattering of grey-shingled beach shacks peering out from the horizon. Then it would be time for the story.

Their very own special Nantucket story.

"Tell me the story again, Mommy, about the time when you were a little girl at the beach. You know the one. The one that Nanny said was a fig ...fig ... fig ..."

"Figment of my imagination?"

Mary Margaret's mother always told her this very special story when they were on the ferry to Nantucket Island. It always made Mary Margaret's heart go Thumpity Thump.

Mary Margaret's mother always began her story when the jetties were coming closer and closer ... when the lighthouse began to get larger and larger ... and when the small grey beach shacks started to look like big homes. She just seemed to understand how special this time was on the Far-a-Away Island, so very far out at sea.

But first she always gave Mary Margaret a kiss on her cheek before she began the tale. This was a special tradition before she told her story.

And so her story began.

Many years ago when I was a little girl, I took this same ferry trip with my mother for our special summer vacation on Nantucket Island. It was our very own mother–daughter time.

We rode our bikes on the bike bath and would yell, "I smell the honeysuckles!" or, "Yes! Yes! I smell the beach roses!" "I see the blueberries!"

Yogurt one day and ice cream the next. We laughed and laughed as our tongues tried to keep up with the cold dripping treat. Ice cream on our noses! Yogurt on our shirts! Sand in our shoes!

We would stroll down Main Street at night and listen to the sidewalk music makers. She would let me toss money into the open guitar cases. People would crowd around with smiles on their faces. I liked to watch the cases fill up with dollar bills.

The best blueberries are on this island. But I really do not like to talk about the time we had blueberry pancakes. The pancakes were delicious and made with the very blueberries I had picked early that morning. They were dripping with melted butter, and smothered with pure maple syrup. Unfortunately, I was also SMOTHERED with poison ivy!

Bumpity, bumpity, bumpity, my bike jiggled and jaggled down the cobblestone streets, always taking me on my way to the penny candy store to spend some of my

allowance. I made sure to always pack some bread in my basket. I would sit on the wharf, swinging my legs and sharing my feast with the screeching seagulls overhead, and the ducks swimming circles beneath my dangling feet. They always seemed to know that I wanted to be fair, but they sometimes had trouble taking turns.

In the evenings we would walk down to the beach when the moon was high and bright in the sky. I watched the fishermen cast their lines into the sea and knew they were catching blue fish. I often wondered if sometimes they caught anything else. One time my mother shouted, "Look! Look! A shooting star! Make a wish and don't tell!" And I did. And I did not tell.

My very favorite and best of all times were the beach times, when I just wandered the beach and looked for shells. Plinkity! Plank! The shells jingled and jangled as I dropped them one by one in my red, shiny bucket.

On my tummy I would lay in the toasty warm sand, just behind the edge of the water. I would wait to see what treasures the ocean waves would leave behind, and then grab back to again take out to sea.

The sun and rhythm of the crashing waves sometimes made me sleepy. My eyes would blur as I lay on the beach with my cheeks touching the damp sand. My mother would often gently wake me with her saltwater kisses on my cheek.

But, Mary Margaret, the time I remember most of all was the time I turned my cheek in the sand, pushed my long sea-soaked straggles of hair away from eyes and mouth, and looked out to the ocean to see a beautiful smiling lady waving at me and flip-flopping all around in the water. She was so silly! I watched her make loops and do tricks in the water. She looked as if she was dancing right on top of the water before she would tumble backwards into the ocean with a powerful kick of her brilliant tail. By the time I waved back she had already disappeared somewhere below the ocean surface and I felt very sad. I was hoping she would be my friend that summer.

As I walked back to my blanket, I noticed the most beautiful white, pearly clamshell. Nestled right inside was piece of colored glass. The glass was the color of the ocean on a stormy day. The edges were worn smooth and the middle had a slight ripple that looked like a teeny tiny wave.

Sea glass! I was so excited! I remembered reading about the legend of sea glass. Mermaids' tears made sea glass, and lucky was the sailor that found any. Good luck would keep him safe and stay with him always wherever he traveled.

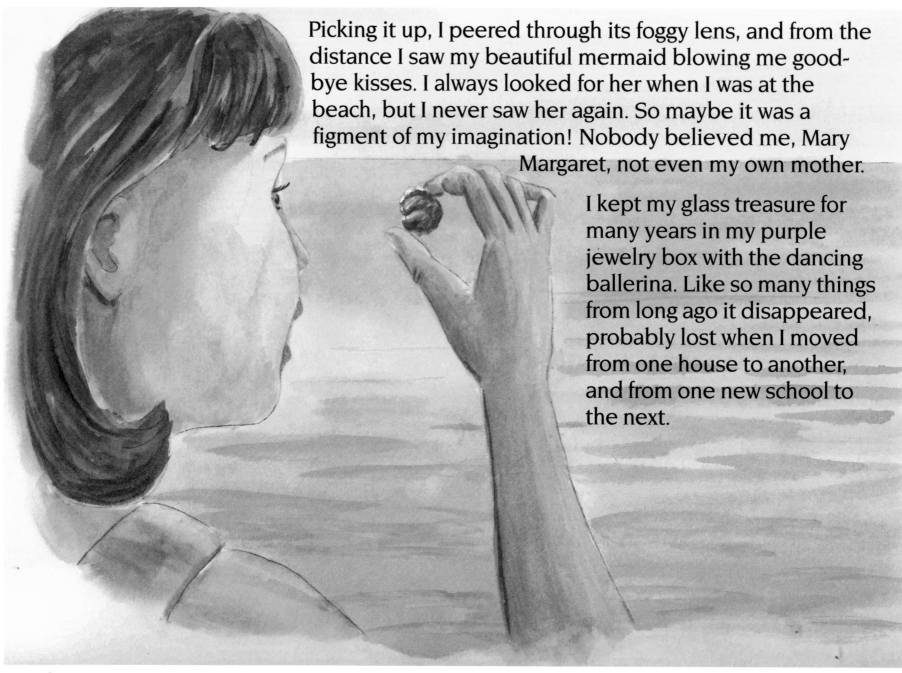

Picking it up, I peered through its foggy lens, and from the distance I saw my beautiful mermaid blowing me good-bye kisses. I always looked for her when I was at the beach, but I never saw her again. So maybe it was a figment of my imagination! Nobody believed me, Mary Margaret, not even my own mother.

I kept my glass treasure for many years in my purple jewelry box with the dancing ballerina. Like so many things from long ago it disappeared, probably lost when I moved from one house to another, and from one new school to the next.

I loved my mother's story and often wondered why she never again saw her beautiful and playful mermaid. I was happy that she was bringing me back to the special place where she spent so many happy summers.

That summer we too biked bumpity bump over the cobblestone streets into town. We sat on the docks and fed the seagulls.

We licked ice cream cones and dripped on our shirts.

We listened to the music makers while strolling on Main Street.

We took deep breaths of honeysuckle and beach roses, as we furiously biked our way to the beach past the colorful blueberry patches.

But we spent most of our time on the beach. My mother read with her legs stretched out from her beach chair so her toes could just reach the cool, sea-foamy sand at the edge of the water. She wore dark sunglasses and her white visor to shade her eyes and face from the hot sun. This was her quiet time.

This was my time to walk on the beach and seek out seashells.

I strolled slowly by screeching boys
as their kites flew out on long,
dangling strings over the ocean.
The colorful kite tails looked as if

they would crash into the sea, but they
dipped and twirled quickly back up as if
they were thrown back into the sky by
invisible hands.

I watched them for a long time, hopping
out of the way when I thought the
stringy tails of the kites would tangle
all around me.

22

Head bent looking for special shells, my toes sank into the warm, tingly sand.

Boat shells, tiger-striped shells, scallop shells, sand dollars, quahogs, and the little gold Jingle bell shells all swished together in

my little bucket. I imagined the beautiful pictures I would paint on the smooth white insides of the big clamshells. They would bring me summer memories on cold winter nights.

knowing that our special days
...t the beach were coming to an
...owly walked back to my blanket.

I counted the ridges
on the fan-shaped
scallop shells.

Sitting at the edge of the water with my toes in the sand, late one afternoon, I gazed out at the sea and that is when I saw her. I held my breath, afraid that if I moved or spoke she would disappear. She looked just as I imagined her, but a whale-shaped shell held back her hair.

Beads of shells on seaweed twisted and coiled all around her neck, over and over and over. She was juggling sand dollars, clamshells, and scallop shells in the water. Around and around they went, with glittering droplets of water sprinkling off of them. Her musical laugh carried all across the waters of the seven seas and called out my name. I looked around but no one else seemed to notice.

"Mom, look!" I cried.

"Yes, it will be a beautiful sunset, Mary Margaret. A perfect sunset for our last summer night at the beach."

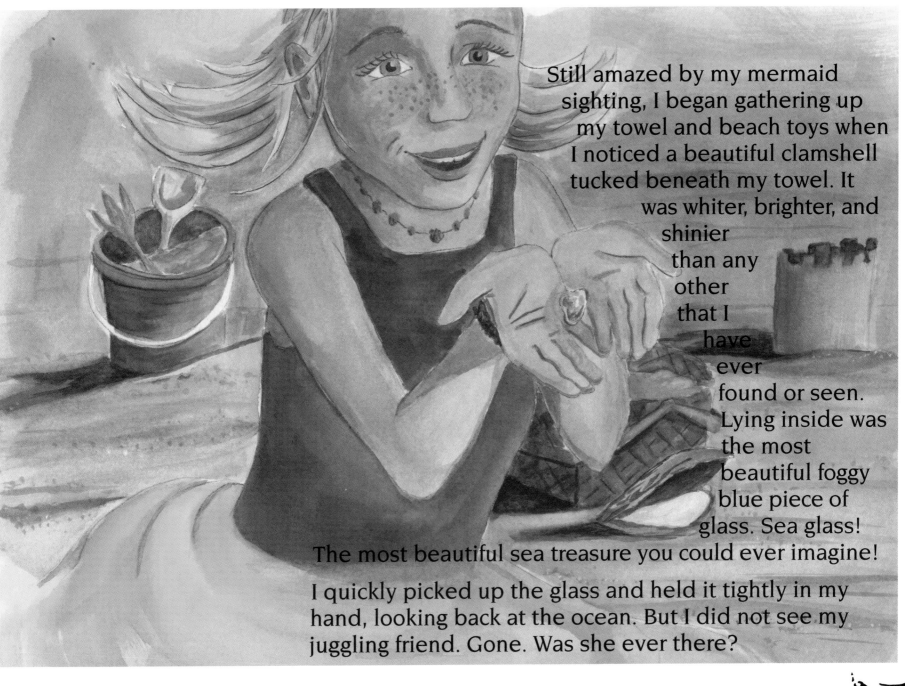

Still amazed by my mermaid sighting, I began gathering up my towel and beach toys when I noticed a beautiful clamshell tucked beneath my towel. It was whiter, brighter, and shinier than any other that I have ever found or seen. Lying inside was the most beautiful foggy blue piece of glass. Sea glass! The most beautiful sea treasure you could ever imagine!

I quickly picked up the glass and held it tightly in my hand, looking back at the ocean. But I did not see my juggling friend. Gone. Was she ever there?

I wished I could stay longer. This was the day that seemed so far away just a short time ago. Gathering our beach items for the final trip to the car, I trudged through the sand, gripping my special summer treasure. I kept stopping and turning to look out at the water growing farther and farther away. Maybe I would see her one last time. I never did.

I stood at the top of the hill and looked down. How quiet and lonely it looked with so many people

gone. I breathed in the crisp sea air and listened as gentle waves tickled the sandy edge.

I knew that school was starting soon. I had so many adventures to share with my friends—stories to tell and treasures to share.

As we quickly packed and rushed to catch the ferry, my heart did not thump loudly with anticipation.

The crowds of people pushed and squashed all around me. My backpack was heavy and stuffed with my summer collections.

I stood at the railing and protected my ears from the ferry's loud horn blast.

I watched the golden dome of the church push away from me, the lighthouse grow smaller, and the grey–shingled beach homes slowly disappear.

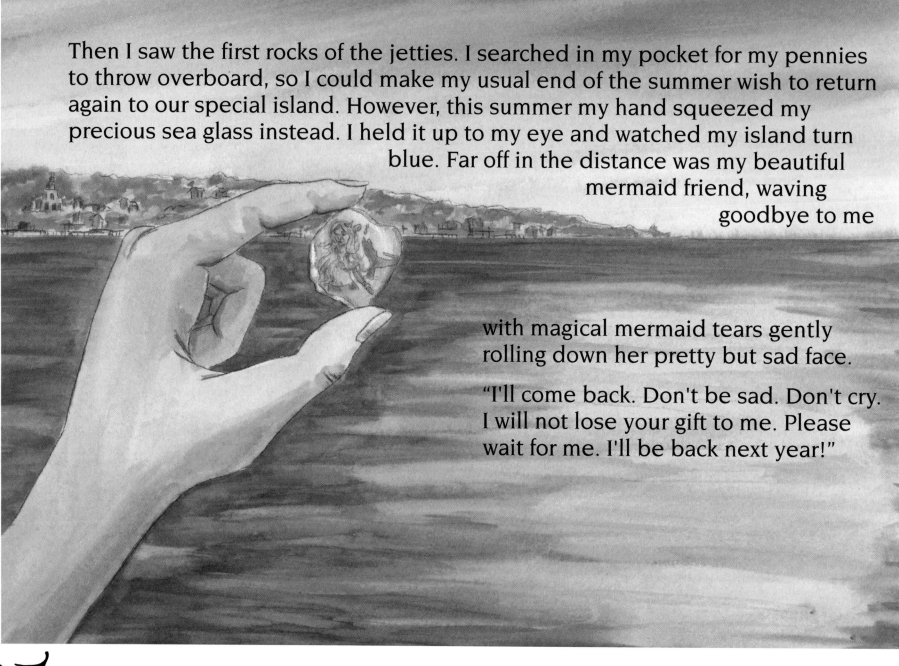

Then I saw the first rocks of the jetties. I searched in my pocket for my pennies to throw overboard, so I could make my usual end of the summer wish to return again to our special island. However, this summer my hand squeezed my precious sea glass instead. I held it up to my eye and watched my island turn blue. Far off in the distance was my beautiful mermaid friend, waving goodbye to me

with magical mermaid tears gently rolling down her pretty but sad face.

"I'll come back. Don't be sad. Don't cry. I will not lose your gift to me. Please wait for me. I'll be back next year!"

I tried to settle in and read the brand new book I had saved for the trip home, but I kept thinking about the following summer when I knew that I would return. Some things would be the same. Some things would be different. I just knew, though, I would see my special friend again, just as I knew that I would discover a lot of beautiful sea glass on my favorite beach. None could ever be as special as the "mermaid tear" left on my blanket, my goodbye gift from my friend from the sea.

My mother leaned down and gently gave me one last salt-water kiss as I looked down at the foggy blue glass in my hand. I could not stop gazing at my magical mermaid's tear; it was my own special promise of next summer.

The End

33

Remember to search for your very own special piece of sea glass the next time you visit the beach, and make sure to think of all the playful mermaids swimming beneath the beautiful waters of our seven seas!